ST?

ALLEN COUNTY PUBLIC LIBRARY

FRIENDS
OF ACPL

P9-BZL-545

MR. PIPER'S BUS

Books by Eleanor Clymer
Chester
Treasure at First Base
A Yard for John
Mr. Piper's Bus

By Eleanor Clymer and Lillian Erlich
Modern American Career Women

*By Eleanor Clymer, Lillian M. Gilbreth
and Orpha Mae Thomas*
Management in the Home

MR. PIPER'S BUS

BY ELEANOR CLYMER

Illustrated by Kurt Wiese

DODD, MEAD & COMPANY, NEW YORK, 1961

j C 629 mi

Copyright © 1961 by Eleanor Clymer
Member, Authors League of America

All rights reserved

No part of this book may be reproduced in any form
without permission in writing from the publisher

Library of Congress Catalog Card Number: 61-6935

Printed in the United States of America
by The Cornwall Press, Inc., Cornwall, N. Y.

1162868

Contents

1. Mr. Piper Has Problems   9
2. Mr. Piper Gets an Idea   20
3. Mr. Piper on the Road   25
4. A Good Home for Buster   29
5. A Home for a Cat and Three Kittens   36
6. Little Mack Finds a Friend   43
7. A Stormy Night   52
8. The Little House on the Mountain   61
9. Down the Mountain   70
10. Home Again   79

MR. PIPER'S BUS

1. Mr. Piper Has Problems

Mr. Hiram Piper was a bus driver. He wore a green uniform. He smoked a pipe. He was short and plump, with gray hair under his green bus-driver's cap.

All day he drove from one end of the city to the other. He enjoyed his job. He liked to see the different people who got on and off the bus. He liked the ladies with shopping bags, going to the stores; he liked the men with briefcases, going to their offices. Most of all, he liked the boys and girls going to school with their books, or to the park with their balls or ropes or hoops.

"Step lively! Plenty of room in the rear!" he called out, in such a cheerful voice that everybody moved right back. He was always cheerful.

Sometimes he even sang. He knew two songs. One was "Sailing, sailing, over the bounding main." The other was "She'll be comin' round the mountain when she comes." He sang softly, of course. The passengers might have thought it strange for a bus driver to sing.

But suddenly Mr. Piper began to feel sad. He wasn't tired. He wasn't sick. He was just sad.

He felt it coming on one day when he heard some boys talking. One said, "We're going to have fun this summer. Our cousins are coming from California. We're going to the beach. We'll have picnics and camping trips. It will be keen."

This made Mr. Piper feel very lonely. He had no cousins. He had no boys and girls of his own. He had no family at all to visit him or go on picnics with him. He had never thought about it before, but now he thought about it all the time. Passengers were all right, and he liked them. But at the end of the day he had nobody to go home to.

He looked so sad that the other bus drivers noticed it. They said he needed a vacation. So Mr. Piper

went to the seashore. He stayed a week, but he felt just as lonely there as he did at home. He came back, feeling worse than ever.

The bus passengers noticed it. They asked one another, "What ever happened to that cheerful man who used to drive this bus?"

Every day Mr. Piper felt sadder. It wasn't surprising. He lived by himself in a small room. In the morning, he fixed his own breakfast and tidied up the place. In the evening, after work, he cooked his lonely dinner. After that, he washed the dishes and then sat in front of his television set until bedtime.

And all day long, he drove his bus filled with people. But he kept thinking that he didn't really know them, and he felt lonelier and lonelier.

Then, suddenly, things started happening.

One evening, when Mr. Piper was coming home from work, he saw a small brown dog running along the street.

The dog had no collar. He ran into every doorway. He ran up to everyone he saw. "Where's my house?" he seemed to be asking.

"Hello there, Buster," said Mr. Piper. "Are you lost?"

"Woof!" said the dog, wagging his stubby tail. And he turned around and ran after Mr. Piper.

Mr. Piper stopped. "Wait a minute," he said. "I didn't say you should come home with me."

The dog came right along. He followed Mr. Piper up the stairs and into his room. He ran all around the place, sniffing. Then he lay down and went to sleep.

When Mr. Piper's supper was ready, the dog woke up.

"Are you hungry, Buster?" Mr. Piper asked.

12

"Woof!" said the dog, sitting up and waving his front paws. He hungrily ate the stew Mr. Piper gave him. He licked the dish clean. Afterward, he went to sleep again, with his chin on Mr. Piper's foot.

The next morning, when Mr. Piper went to work, the little dog stood in the doorway, waving good-by with his tail.

"Good-by, Buster," said Mr. Piper.

In the evening, the dog was there waiting. He jumped up and down joyfully to welcome Mr. Piper home. It was nice, having someone there to come home to.

But Mr. Piper's landlady didn't like it. "No dogs allowed," she said.

"But Buster has no home," said Mr. Piper. "I can't just put him out. And he doesn't bother anyone."

This was true. Buster was very good. Before breakfast and after dinner, Mr. Piper took him for a walk. In the middle of the day, a boy who lived next door came and took him out. The rest of the time, Buster slept, or looked out of the window at the people in the street.

Then something else happened. One day, when Mr. Piper reached home, he found a gray cat with white feet sitting on the rug in his room.

13

"Hello, Mrs. Cat," said Mr. Piper. "Where did you come from?"

The cat didn't say. She rubbed herself against his leg, purring loudly.

"Either Buster opened the door for you, or you came in through the window," said Mr. Piper.

"Meow!" said the cat.

She ate the supper Mr. Piper gave her. Then she jumped into his lap and went to sleep.

The landlady didn't like that, either. "No cats allowed," she said.

"All right," said Mr. Piper. "Just let her stay until I can find a home for her."

14

"Well, don't take too long about it," said the land-lady crossly.

Mr. Piper asked a few people if they wanted a gray cat with white feet. But nobody did, so the cat stayed.

It was nice having Buster and Mrs. Cat to welcome him home.

"What would they do without me?" Mr. Piper wondered, as he opened cans of cat and dog food. "And what would I do without them?"

Then another thing happened. Mr. Piper got Little Mack. Little Mack was a chicken.

It happened this way. Two girls were riding on the bus one day. One of them had a basket.

"I have two baby chickens in this basket," she said, "I'm taking them to show my teacher."

"May I see them?" her friend asked.

They opened the basket and looked inside.

"Oh, how darling!" said the friend. "And aren't they little!"

"They are bantam chicks," said the girl who owned them.

Just then the bus jerked, and she dropped the basket. The chicks fell out. The girls found one of them, but the other was not to be seen. They had to

15

get off without it. Later, when the bus was empty, Mr. Piper heard a faint noise under a seat.

"Peep! Peep!"

He reached down and pulled out a little yellow ball of fluff.

"Well, Mack, what were you doing there?" Mr. Piper asked. "That is no place for a little fellow like you."

The chick pecked at his finger with a tiny, tiny beak. "Peep! Peep!" it cried.

Mr. Piper put it carefully into his coat pocket and took it home.

"This is Mack," he said to Buster and Mrs. Cat, "though I suppose I should call him *Little* Mack. You must be nice to him."

He made a house for Little Mack out of a cardboard box. He fed him bread and milk and bits of lettuce and apple. Little Mack grew, although he never got very big. He was a bantam, and bantam chickens don't grow big. He did grow feathers and a fine red comb. When Mr. Piper sat in front of the television set in the evening, Little Mack flew up and perched on the back of his chair. Buster sat at his feet, and Mrs. Cat snoozed in his lap.

Mr. Piper didn't feel lonely any more. He was very happy. "What would they do without me?" he asked. "And what did I ever do without them?"

When the landlady found out there was a chicken in Mr. Piper's room, she was very angry.

"No chickens allowed in here," she exclaimed.

"But this chicken isn't bothering anyone," said Mr. Piper.

"No chickens!" declared the landlady firmly.

Mr. Piper promised to find a home for Little Mack. But before he could do so, something happened.

One morning he was awakened by a loud voice calling, "Cock-a-doodle-doo!"

17

Little Mack had grown up. He was a rooster, and roosters crow in the morning.

Mr. Piper jumped out of bed. "Quiet!" he whispered. "The landlady will hear you!"

"Cock-a-doodle-doo!" crowed Little Mack again.

The landlady did hear him. There she was at the door, hands on hips.

"What's this?" she cried. "No roosters allowed here! You'll have to move this very day!"

"But where shall I go?" Mr. Piper asked.

"How about the zoo?" the landlady suggested. She was very angry.

"Please!" Mr. Piper begged. "You must give me a couple of days. I can't just pack up and move now. I have to go to work. I'll lose my job if I don't."

"All right. Two days. No more," said the landlady.

Mr. Piper dressed himself and fed his animals. He went to work with a heavy heart. Where could he go? He would have to give away his animals. But who would take them?

He asked the other bus drivers. But none of them wanted a dog, a cat or a rooster.

At five o'clock he hurried home. There was another surprise. Three tiny new voices said, "Mew! Mew! Mew!"

Mrs. Cat looked up at him, purring proudly. She had kittens.

"This is the end!" Mr. Piper groaned. "What am I going to do now?"

19

2. Mr. Piper Gets an Idea

That evening, as Mr. Piper sat in front of his television set, he was so worried that he hardly saw the picture. But suddenly, on the screen, he noticed something. There was a picture of a farm. The farmer was going to the barn. A dog and a cat were following him. Chickens were pecking in the yard.

"That's it!" exclaimed Mr. Piper. "I'll take you all to a farm. I'll be lonesome, but that can't be helped. Maybe I'll get used to it."

The next day he went to his boss. "I must have a week's vacation," he said.

"But you just had a vacation," his boss reminded him.

"I'm sorry," said Mr. Piper. "This is very important. I've got to have another."

"You can't take one vacation right after another," the boss told him.

"This is an emergency," Mr. Piper explained. "If you don't let me go, I'll just have to leave."

"Is it a family matter?" the boss asked.

"Yes, it is," Mr. Piper answered.

"Well, all right," said the boss. "I suppose it can't be helped. We'll make an exception in your case."

Mr. Piper hurried home. Now the question was, how to get his animals to the farm. And what farm? He didn't even know where he was going.

"I ought to have an automobile," he thought. "I'll see if I can buy an old car."

He went to the bank and took out the money he had saved. Then he went to a place where old automobiles were sold. He looked at all the cars in the lot. Some were too big. Some were too small. Some were too expensive.

At last, far back in a corner of the lot, he saw an old green bus. It was small and battered and rusty. But Mr. Piper liked it.

"A bus is what I need," he thought. "I'm a bus driver, after all. This will be just right—if it does not cost too much, and if it runs."

The price was low, so Mr. Piper drove the bus around the block a few times, poked at it, and looked under the hood.

"I'll take it," he said.

All Mr. Piper's neighbors were surprised to see an old green bus parked in front of the house. But he didn't notice. He ran up the stairs as fast as he could go.

"We're going away," he told his animals.

"Meow?" said Mrs. Cat.

"Yes, you and all your kittens," said Mr. Piper.

22

"Now don't worry. I'll take care of everything. You just get your children ready."

Of course, the animals really had nothing to get ready. Mr. Piper put his clothes into a bag. Then he thought, "I wonder where we will sleep if I don't find a place the first day. They won't let me into a hotel with all these animals. I'll take my blankets and pillows. Then I can sleep in the bus." He looked around the room. "I'll take my folding table and chair. I may want to sit under a tree somewhere."

He carried the things down to the bus. Then he thought, "I may as well take my dishes and my pots and pans. I might want to do my own cooking."

He wondered whether to take his television set. "I won't take that," he decided. "There's no place to connect it, and anyway, I'll be too busy to watch it."

23

He picked up his bus-driver's cap and put it on his head. "I'm still a bus driver," he said, looking down at his green uniform.

He carried Little Mack and the kittens down to the bus. Buster and Mrs. Cat followed. Mr. Piper sat down behind the steering wheel. He was just about to drive off, when his landlady came running out.

"Where are you going?" she demanded.

"I'm going to find a home for my animals," Mr. Piper told her.

"Well, don't forget to come back," she said. "I'll be glad to have you—without your animals."

"I'll see about it," said Mr. Piper.

"Woof, woof!" said Buster.

"Cock-a-doodle-doo!" crowed Little Mack.

"Meow!" said Mrs. Cat.

"Mew! Mew! Mew!" cried the kittens, crawling about in their box.

And off they went.

3. Mr. Piper on the Road

It was a beautiful summer day. The sun shone down brightly on the streets and buildings, on the people and cars hurrying along.

Buster sat on the front seat, with his head out of the window. Mrs. Cat sat on the next seat. Little Mack perched on the back of the third seat. They all seemed to be enjoying the ride.

Mr. Piper began to enjoy it, too. "This will be fun," he told the animals. "We'll see the country. Afterward, I'll find good homes for you. You'll like it."

"Meow!" said Mrs. Cat, jumping down into the box with her kittens.

25

"Don't worry," said Mr. Piper. "Nobody is going to take them away from you. Please stop worrying."

He had been worrying himself. But now he felt much better. He began to sing:

> "Sailing, sailing, over the bounding main,
> And many a stormy wind shall blow e'er
> Jack comes home again!"

He sang as loudly as he could. This was his own bus, and he could sing loudly if he wanted to. But where was the bounding main? Oh, here it was! They came to a bridge over a river. They crossed the bridge and found themselves on a broad highway.

On both sides were gas stations and diners. A sign said, "EAT!" Mr. Piper was hungry. He had been so excited about leaving that he had forgotten about lunch. He stopped the bus.

"Wait here!" he told the animals.

He went in and got three hamburgers, a bottle of milk, some lettuce, some coffee and a pie. He took the food out to the bus and they all had lunch.

"This is expensive, though," he said. "I'll have to find a cheaper way of eating."

When they came to a grocery store, Mr. Piper stopped again. He bought some canned cat and dog food, some bread and cheese and fruit, some corn for Little Mack, and some milk.

"Now we're all set," he said.

They left the gas stations and diners behind. Soon they were in the country. There were fields, farmhouses and barns. It looked like the picture on the television screen.

"Only it's better," said Mr. Piper. "It smells good."

Farmers were cutting hay. Apples were ripening on the trees. Mr. Piper turned off into a side road. The sun was beginning to go down. The sky was pink in the west. Long shadows lay across the road.

Mr. Piper yawned. "I'm getting tired," he said. "Let's spend the night under this apple tree."

The animals seemed to like the idea. Mr. Piper parked the bus well off the road. He opened the door and let Buster and Mrs. Cat out.

"You go for a walk while I'm getting supper," he told them. "But don't go far."

He tied a long string to Little Mack's leg, so he would not get lost. Little Mack walked around, pecking at bugs and pebbles. He seemed to know just what to do, even though he had been raised in the city.

Mr. Piper took out his folding table and chair. He

put out the food he had bought and sprinkled corn on the ground for Little Mack.

After supper, they all rested quietly. Mr. Piper smoked his pipe. Buster lay at his feet. Little Mack roosted in the apple tree. Mrs. Cat sat in Mr. Piper's lap, just as if she were at home.

The sky turned deep blue, and then black. The stars twinkled, and a little moon shone. Crickets chirped, and now and then a bird called. Mrs. Cat went into the bus to feed her children.

Mr. Piper went in, too, to make his bed. Then he had an idea. "Why shouldn't I sleep outdoors? The night is warm, and it doesn't look like rain."

He made up his bed under the tree and lay down. Buster curled up at his feet. A breeze whispered in the leaves.

"This is good!" said Mr. Piper. A minute later, he was asleep.

28

4. A Good Home for Buster

A loud voice woke Mr. Piper.

"Cock-a-doodle-doo!"

He sat up and tried to jump out of bed. But where was he? Instead of a floor under his feet, there were grass and pebbles. Instead of a ceiling overhead, there were leafy branches. Instead of an alarm clock ringing, there was a little rooster up in a tree.

"Moo!" said another voice close by.

A brown cow was staring at Mr. Piper with big, dark eyes. Buster jumped up and began to bark.

Mr. Piper said, "Be quiet, Buster. That's a cow." Then he explained to the cow, "Buster is a city dog.

He never saw a cow before. Where did you come from?"

"Moo!" said the cow again. Mr. Piper could see that her bag was big and full. He didn't know much about cows, either, but he thought she wanted to be milked.

"Well, I don't know how to milk you," he said. "Why don't you go home where you belong?"

"Mooooooooo-oo!" said the cow.

Mr. Piper put on his shoes and walked up a little hill in the middle of the field. From there, he could see a farm down on the other side.

"That must be where you live," he said to the cow. But he didn't know how to get her to go there.

30

Suddenly Buster began to bark. "Woof! Woof!" He ran at the cow and nipped her. It wasn't a hard nip, but the cow began to move toward the farm.

"Why, Buster!" exclaimed Mr. Piper. "How smart you are! I didn't know you could drive cows!"

The cow walked down the hill to the barnyard, with Buster after her. Mr. Piper followed.

"Is this your cow?" he asked the farmer who came out of the barn.

"Yes, she is," answered the farmer. "Thanks for bringing her back. Where did you find her?"

"I camped over the hill last night," Mr. Piper told him. "She came around this morning, to see what we were doing. I saw your farm, so my dog and I brought her here."

"Thanks a lot," said the farmer. "Would you like some fresh milk?"

Mr. Piper was glad to have the milk. It was still warm, and it smelled good. Everything about the farm seemed good. It looked so peaceful and busy. The chickens clucked in their yard. The pigs grunted. The ducks waggled their tails as they swam in the pond. A cat came out of the barn, followed by two kittens.

But there didn't seem to be any dog. Suddenly Mr. Piper had an idea. This might be the right place for Buster.

He hadn't planned to give Buster away so soon, but it did seem like a good chance.

"Would you like to have a dog?" he asked. "I'm looking for a home for Buster."

The farmer seemed surprised, but he said, "Why, yes, I do need a dog. I don't have a dog now. As a matter of fact, I have been looking for one."

"Of course, Buster is a city dog," said Mr. Piper. "But he does seem to be smart."

"Oh, he's smart, all right," said the farmer. "I saw the way he drove the cow down here. He could be trained easily."

Buster knew they were talking about him. He wagged his tail proudly and said, "Woof!"

"All right," said the farmer, patting Buster. "I'll take him, if you're sure you want to give him away."

"I don't want to," said Mr. Piper. "But I have to. I live in the city and I can't keep him there."

The farmer nodded. He called to his wife, "Here's a new dog! Will you please take him inside and feed him? His name is Buster."

"Here, Buster!" called the farmer's wife.

Buster ran happily to the kitchen door. Mr. Piper watched him go inside. Then he turned away.

"Take good care of him," he called over his shoulder.

He hurried to his bus. He put Little Mack, Mrs. Cat and the kittens and all his things inside as fast as he could. Then he started the motor. He wanted to get away before Buster noticed that he was gone.

"Meow!" said Mrs. Cat. She ran up and down the aisle, looking on all the seats. "Meow!" she said again.

"Are you looking for Buster? I found him a good home. He's going to be very happy there. Don't

33

worry about him," said Mr. Piper, as he stared at the road and pressed his foot hard on the gas pedal.

But he couldn't help worrying himself. No Buster! No little dog to lick his face in the morning and jump for joy when he came home at night! And what would Buster think when he found Mr. Piper gone? He'd think his master didn't love him any more! Mr. Piper felt so badly that he had to stop the bus and blow his nose.

He was just giving one last blow, when he looked into his rearview mirror. Far back on the road he saw a small cloud of dust. It was coming nearer. What could it be? Something was running on the road.

He started the bus. "I won't look," he thought as he drove ahead. But he couldn't help looking. Now

34

it was not a cloud of dust. It was a small brown spot. It was a dog, running as fast as it could, with tongue hanging out and ears flapping. It was Buster!

Mr. Piper stopped the bus again. Buster galloped up. He leaped up the steps and jumped into Mr. Piper's lap. He licked his face all over and sang through his nose with joy. 1162868

"Hooray! I found you!" he seemed to be saying. "You got lost, but don't worry! I'll always find you!"

He wiggled and waggled until he fell on the floor. He jumped right up again. "My, I was scared!" he seemed to say. "I thought I'd have to stay on that farm forever!"

"What will the farmer think?" asked Mr. Piper.

Buster didn't seem to care what the farmer would think. He licked Mr. Piper's face again.

"*Pfoo!* Stop that and listen to me," said Mr. Piper.

"Yip! Yip!" yelped Buster.

Mrs. Cat came running up and licked his nose. "You be more careful next time. We almost went off without you," she seemed to be telling him.

Mr. Piper sighed. "The way you chased that cow," he said, "I thought you'd be happy on the farm. But maybe you are a city dog, after all. Very well, I'll take you back and find you a home in the city."

5. *A Home for a Cat and Three Kittens*

They traveled on all day. Mr. Piper couldn't help feeling glad to have Buster back. He liked to see him sitting up on the front seat with his head out of the window and his ears flapping in the breeze.

"But I *will* have to do something about Mrs. Cat and the kittens," he said. "I hope *they* won't mind living in the country."

That evening, while Mr. Piper was getting supper ready, Mrs. Cat went hunting. She came back with a fine, fat mouse which she put down at his feet.

"For you," she seemed to be saying.

"Thanks very much," said Mr. Piper. "Another time. You keep this one."

To himself he said, "Some farmer should be glad to have a cat like that."

The next morning he began looking for a good place for Mrs. Cat and her kittens. He pulled up in front of a red farmhouse with a big front yard.

"This looks very nice," he told Mrs. Cat. "You'll like it." But when the farmer's wife came out and heard his story, she shook her head.

"I'm sorry," she told him. "I already have a mother cat, two big kittens and three little kittens."

At the next house, a very nice little girl came out.

She said she would be glad to have Mrs. Cat and the kittens. She was just carrying the kittens inside, when her mother came out.

"Sally!" she exclaimed. "You know we have three cats already. I've told you and told you, no more cats!"

"What am I to do?" poor Mr. Piper asked. "I must find a home for my cats."

"Why don't you take them to the county fair?" Sally's mother suggested. "It is going on in town now. People often give away kittens at the fair."

Mr. Piper drove to the village. Gay flags were everywhere. There were games and sideshows and a merry-go-round. People were arriving in cars and trucks, bringing farm animals, vegetables, jars of fruit, pies and bed quilts. Sure enough, some people had kittens and puppies to give away.

Mr. Piper parked his bus with the other cars. He put Mrs. Cat into the box with her kittens. Then he carried them to the building where the other people were taking their puppies and kittens.

The lady in charge looked very doubtful. "They're very pretty kittens," she said, "but it's hard to get rid of a cat with kittens. Still, you can put them there, and maybe someone will want them. You might go

round the fair and come back later. We'll let you know if anyone wants them."

Mr. Piper put the box down. He patted Mrs. Cat.

"You purr and be as nice as you can," he said. "Then somebody will want you *and* the kittens."

Then he walked away as quickly as he could. He tried to get interested in the fair. He looked at all the wonderful cakes and pies.

"If I felt hungry," he said to himself, "these things would look mighty good."

He decided to buy a pie and some cookies, in case he got hungry later. He took a ride on the Ferris wheel, but somehow he didn't enjoy it.

He thought of Mrs. Cat, all alone with her kittens among a lot of strangers, and he felt very sad. He decided to go and see how she was getting along.

He went back to the building where he had left her, but she wasn't there. The box was empty!

The lady in charge came to talk to him. "Somebody must have taken your cats," she said. "I didn't see them go, but they aren't here now."

"Well," said Mr. Piper, "I hope it was some nice person who took them. I hope they'll be happy."

He went sadly back to his bus. The door was open.

"I thought I shut that," he said. "I wonder if any-

40

one has been here." But everything looked all right. Buster and Little Mack were glad to see him.

"I brought you something," he said, giving each of them a cookie. He started the bus and was just backing out of the parking lot, when he heard a voice saying, "Meow!"

And there was Mrs. Cat, walking down the aisle.

"How did *you* get here?" he asked. "Who opened the door for you? And where are the kittens?"

Just then he heard some little voices saying, "Mew! Mew! Mew! Mew!" He got up and went to look.

41

There were the kittens under a seat. Mrs. Cat must have carried them, one at a time, all the way from the fair! One, two, three—why, there were *four* of them! Mrs. Cat's three gray kittens—and a black one!

"Wait a minute! This one isn't yours!" he said. "Where did you get him?"

Mrs. Cat stood there purring. "I adopted him," she seemed to be saying. "Isn't he cute?"

"He's cute, all right," said Mr. Piper. "But what am I going to do with him? It's hard enough to get rid of three kittens. Four will be even worse."

Mrs. Cat didn't seem a bit worried. She just looked pleased.

"Don't *you* want to live in the country either?" Mr. Piper asked her. "It would be so good for the children."

Mrs. Cat rubbed herself against his legs and purred. Then she lay down to give the kittens their supper.

Mr. Piper sighed. What could anyone do with a cat like that? Shaking his head, he got back behind the wheel, and they started off again.

6. *Little Mack Finds a Friend*

It was nice to have Mrs. Cat back, even with an extra kitten. The black kitten was older and bigger than Mrs. Cat's babies. They still had their eyes closed, but his were open, and he could see what went on around him. He kept getting out of the box. Mrs. Cat had to keep running after him and putting him back.

When they stopped for the night, Mr. Piper took him outdoors and he at once began to climb a tree. Mrs. Cat was so worried that Mr. Piper had to help her. He got the black kitten down and put it in his pocket. Then it began to climb up his coat. Finally,

Mr. Piper put it into the bus and shut the door and all the windows.

"It serves you right," he told Mrs. Cat. "You had plenty to do with three children. You shouldn't have adopted a fourth. And such a bad child, too!"

"Prrrr!" said Mrs. Cat. "You know how children are. He'll outgrow it."

The next morning, Mr. Piper decided to do something about Little Mack. Three days of his week were gone, and he still had all his animals, plus an extra kitten.

But surely a rooster should be happy in the country. Little Mack seemed to love sleeping in a tree and scratching in the dirt for bugs and pebbles.

Mr. Piper looked at all the farms he passed. Most of them had chickens. But the chickens were all so big! How could he leave his little bantam among them?

At last, at the side of the road, he saw a little brown hen walking daintily among the leaves. She was smaller than Little Mack!

Little Mack saw her, too. "Cock-a-doodle-doo!" he crowed, flapping his wings. Then out through the

44

open window he flew. He landed in the grass beside her. The little hen walked away.

Little Mack followed. He scratched up a worm and stepped back to let her see it. The hen gobbled it up. After that, they walked side by side.

"Little Mack has found a friend," said Mr. Piper. "This ought to be a good place to leave him."

He drove on to the house. Several more bantam hens were walking about. One had a brood of chicks, tiny yellow balls of fluff, with legs like toothpicks.

"Cluck, cluck!" said the mother, gathering her babies about her.

"Don't worry, I won't hurt them," Mr. Piper told her.

A beautiful little rooster with shiny tail feathers sat on a fence and flapped his wings.

Mr. Piper knocked at the door. "I'm looking for a home for a bantam rooster," he told the lady who

45

answered. "I live in the city and can't keep him there. I see you have bantams."

"I have a good many bantams," said the lady. "I'll be glad to take your rooster, if he can get along with mine. Roosters sometimes fight, you know."

"Here comes Little Mack now," said Mr. Piper.

Little Mack and the brown hen came through the bushes side by side, talking in a friendly way.

The other rooster flew down from the fence. He walked up to Little Mack. Both of them fluffed up their feathers and stared at each other. They walked around in a circle. Then, with a squawk, they jumped at each other.

"Cluck, cluck, cluck!" exclaimed the mother hen to her children, and they all scurried out of the way.

Squawk! Again the two roosters jumped at each other. Some feathers flew into the air, and Little Mack flapped his wings. The other rooster walked away. Little Mack had won!

"Cock-a-doodle-doo!" he crowed. The little brown hen walked up to him admiringly.

The woman laughed. "Your rooster will be all right here," she said.

"Well, I'll be going then," said Mr. Piper. He walked to the bus. When he looked back, Little Mack and the brown hen were strolling about happily.

Mr. Piper drove away. Not far down the road, he came to a meadow. A brook ran through it. He parked his bus and began to fix supper. Buster and Mrs. Cat came running when he called them. But Buster was worried. He looked around and said, "Woof!" He ran back to the bus and looked inside.

47

He came back to Mr. Piper and said "Woof!" again.

"If you are looking for Little Mack," said Mr. Piper, "he is not going to be with us any more. He, at least, has sense enough to know when he has a good home."

Buster made a noise that sounded like "Hmff!" Mrs. Cat walked away and began to give her children their baths. They seemed to be cross with him for leaving Little Mack behind.

"Well, it can't be helped," said Mr. Piper.

After supper, he sat and smoked his pipe. The brook rippled through the meadow. Swallows swooped through the air, catching bugs for their supper. The stars came out.

Mr. Piper wondered what Little Mack was doing. Was he happy with his new friends? Would he find a good place to sleep? Would he get along with the other rooster?

At last Mr. Piper fell asleep.

In the morning, he heard a voice calling, "Cock-a-doodle-doo!"

"I'm dreaming," he said.

Then another voice said, "Cluck, cluck, cluck!"

There was Little Mack, sitting in the tree over Mr. Piper's head. Beside him was the little brown hen!

48

Here was a fine howdy-do! Mr. Piper looked up at the two birds angrily.

"Well!" he scolded Little Mack. "Is this the thanks I get for finding you a good home? You don't want to live with the nice lady and all the other bantams? You think you're a city rooster, is that it? And you want to take your lady friend home to the city, too!"

Little Mack said something Mr. Piper couldn't understand.

"I suppose you think I am going to take care of you the rest of your life!" Mr. Piper went on. "Well, I'm not. I've got to go home and I can't take you with me. Roosters can't live in the city. Do you hear?"

Little Mack didn't seem to think he had done anything wrong. He flew down and landed in front of Mr. Piper.

"Cut-cut?" he said.

"Now I suppose you want breakfast," said Mr. Piper. "Well, all right. Nobody else can eat this corn anyway."

He sprinkled corn on the ground. Little Mack called up to the hen, "Cut-cut-cut!"

She flew down and began to eat the corn, while Little Mack watched her proudly. They looked so pretty that Mr. Piper didn't have the heart to scold them any more.

Buster came running out of the bus. He ran up to the hen and sniffed her. She jumped back with a loud squawk, but Little Mack said, "Cut-cut-cut!" in a reassuring voice, as if he were telling her that Buster was a friend.

Mrs. Cat came galloping through the long grass. Mr. Piper looked down at his little family.

"So here we are, back together again," he said. "Very well. We'll go on a little longer. Maybe something will turn up."

He packed up and drove to the nearest village. There he sent a telegram to his boss.

"Must take one more week. Family business not settled yet."

Then he bought some gas and some groceries, and off they all went.

7. A Stormy Night

And now the road went up, up, up into the hills. Higher and higher the old bus climbed. It puffed and chugged. Mr. Piper wasn't used to hills. In the city he drove along level pavements. *Wheeze! Puff, puff! Chug, chug!* More and more slowly went the bus. At last they came out on a level place. Mr. Piper stopped the bus to give it a rest.

They were on top of a mountain. He could see far, far down over the valley they had left. On the other side was another valley, and more hills. It was beautiful. It made Mr. Piper want to sing.

"She'll be comin' round the mountain when she comes!" he sang as he started off again.

Down, down, down they went. The animals took naps. They were not interested in scenery.

They stopped for lunch by the side of the road. All around were cool, shady woods. A brook tumbled down the hill. Birds called. The air smelled of pine trees.

After lunch they went on again. Up and up they went now. There were no houses. They were all alone among the hills.

"She'll be comin' round the mountain when she comes!" Mr. Piper warbled as they started downhill once more. "We'll have chicken and dumplings when

she comes!'" He stopped singing quickly as the thought came to him that the bantams might not like those words. But they had not noticed.

And now Mr. Piper began to look for a place to stop for the night. The woods were thicker and deeper than before. The road was rough and stony. The old bus rattled and banged.

Suddenly, it began to grow dark. Gray clouds covered the sky.

"Guess we'll have a storm," Mr. Piper said, wondering what it would be like to be caught in a storm in the mountains.

"Meow!" said Mrs. Cat, running to her box and licking her babies.

"Well, it's nothing to worry about," said Mr. Piper. "We'll just stay in the bus and keep dry."

Thunder rumbled far away. A streak of lightning split the sky. Mr. Piper stopped the bus.

"We may as well stay here," he said. "We'll have a cold supper, as I can't make a fire. Then we'll go to bed early."

As a matter of fact, the two bantams had gone to bed already. To them, the dark sky meant it was night.

Mr. Piper opened cans of pet food for his cat and dog, and made sandwiches for himself.

"*Crash!*" went the thunder. The wind blew the treetops back and forth. Then down came the rain.

It pattered on the leaves at first. Then it came pouring onto the roof of the bus. Water streamed down the windows. It ran in rivers down the road.

"This is quite a storm!" said Mr. Piper.

Buster growled.

"It's nothing to worry about," Mr. Piper said. "Relax."

Mrs. Cat washed her babies anxiously.

"If you really want to get them clean," said Mr. Piper, "you might put them out in the rain." Mrs. Cat did not appreciate the joke.

"Well, thank goodness, it's dry in here," said Mr. Piper. Just at that moment something hit him on the nose. It was a drop of water! He rubbed his nose. The roof was leaking! Another drop came . . . and then another!

"Did I say it was dry in here?" he asked. "Everybody move to the back of the bus."

Then he laughed. It seemed a long time since he had said that to his passengers.

But it was just as wet in the back. The whole roof leaks.

"I should have brought an umbrella," said Mr. Piper. He spread a blanket like a tent across the backs of two seats, and they all crouched underneath.

"It's just a summer shower," he said. "It won't last." But the rain went on and on. The bus got wetter and wetter.

"We can't stay here," said Mr. Piper. "Even if it stops soon, we can't sleep in this wet bus. We'll have to drive on."

He thought of going back. But he remembered that he had not passed any houses for a long time. Maybe there would be some ahead.

He started the motor and pulled out into the road. Just as he did so, a terrific crash of thunder came. It sounded very close. Mr. Piper looked around. Behind the bus, across the road, was a big tree. The storm had knocked it down. That settled it. He couldn't go back. He would have to go on.

The tires spun around on the stony road. Up, up, up they went, while the rain poured down. The water ran down Mr. Piper's neck. The animals crouched under the seats.

"Kachoo!" Buster sneezed.

56

"Don't you go and catch cold," Mr. Piper scolded. "I don't want any sick animals on my hands."

He bent over his steering wheel and peered out through the windshield. He could hardly see through the driving rain. At last they got to the top of the mountain, and started going downhill, skidding on the loose stones.

The sky was getting darker and darker. Night was coming on.

"Doesn't anybody live in this part of the world?" Mr. Piper wondered. He looked in vain for a light. All he could see was the road ahead of him, lit up by his headlights.

He was about to decide they would have to drive all night, or sleep in a very damp bus, when he saw something that looked like a house.

All he could see of it was the edge of the roof against the stormy sky. He swung the bus around so that his headlights could shine on the house. It was a tiny cabin, perched on the hillside.

"Looks as if they've all gone to bed," he said. "Well, I'll have to wake them up."

He stopped the bus, took a flashlight and climbed out. He walked through the long, wet grass in the yard. The trees dripped on him. He stepped up on the little porch.

58

"*Oops!*" he exclaimed, as his foot went through a board in the floor.

"These folks don't take very good care of their place," he said. "Anybody home?"

He knocked on the door. There was no answer. He knocked harder. Still no answer.

"All gone away," he thought. Shining his flashlight, he peered in through a window. The room inside was empty, except for a crooked table and a bed, and an old chair without a seat.

"If we could just get inside and keep dry, it would be a help," said Mr. Piper. He tried the doorknob.

With a loud creak, the door swung open, and he walked in.

"Anybody home?" he shouted, just to make sure. The only sound was the scurrying noise of a mouse running away.

Mr. Piper ran back to the bus. He picked up the box of kittens and carried it into the cabin. Buster and Mrs. Cat ran after him. Then he went back for the bantams. They were very sleepy. Mr. Piper perched them on the back of the chair, and they snuggled together and went back to sleep.

Mrs. Cat shook the water off her paws. Buster shook himself all over. Mr. Piper looked around. There was a fireplace. There were some sticks of wood.

He made a fire. He spread out his blankets to dry. He and Buster and Mrs. Cat sat in front of the fire until they were warm and dry. Then Mr. Piper rolled up in his blankets, lay down on the floor, and went to sleep.

8. *The Little House on the Mountain*

Mr. Piper woke up feeling rather stiff, and wondered where he was. He heard Little Mack crowing somewhere. He heard the kittens squeaking. He opened his eyes and sat up. Why, he had been sleeping on the floor in a little bare, dusty house. Now he remembered. They had come in last night out of the rain. But where was everybody?

He got up and looked around. The little house had only one room. There was a cupboard with some chipped dishes. The bed in the corner had a broken spring, and was covered with an old patchwork quilt. There was a rusty stove, but no sink. One window was broken, and the wind had blown ashes and rain all over the floor. Evidently, nobody had taken care of the house in a long time.

The door had swung open in the night. Buster and Mrs. Cat had gone out somewhere. So had Mr. and Mrs. Mack. The adopted kitten had crawled out of the box and was staggering around on the porch. He was just about to fall into the hole where Mr. Piper had put his foot through a board the night before.

Mr. Piper rescued him. "Somebody ought to fix that," he thought.

The sky was blue overhead. In front of the house there was a big maple tree. The wind blew its branches about, and a shower of drops fell down. From the porch, Mr. Piper could see across a valley to a row of hills beyond. Early morning fog lay in the valley, like a milky lake. The sky beyond the hills was pink.

As he watched, the pink changed to gold, and the sun came up. It flashed on the raindrops and made them shine like diamonds in the tall grass.

Through the grass, like a tiger creeping through

the jungle, came Mrs. Cat, carrying a mouse in her mouth.

Around the corner of the house came Buster, galloping and wagging his tail. He jumped up on Mr. Piper, getting him all wet.

"Cock-a-doodle-doo!" crowed Little Mack from a fence post. But where was Mrs. Mack? Just then, from behind the house, came a voice: "Cut-cut-cut-cudaaaa-cut!"

Mr. Piper went to see where she was. In a tumbledown shed were some old nests. Mrs. Mack had laid an egg in one of them! She squawked proudly as Mr. Piper picked it up.

"You've all made yourself at home, haven't you?" he said, holding the warm little egg in his hand. "May I have this for my breakfast?"

"Wow, wow!" barked Buster, pulling him by the trouser leg.

"Oh, you want your breakfast, too!" said Mr. Piper.

He brought the box of groceries from the bus, and they ate breakfast out on the porch in the sunshine. Mrs. Cat fed her kittens. Buster began to dig a hole near the maple tree. Mr. and Mrs. Mack walked about looking for bugs.

63

"You all seem to think this is where we are going to stay," said Mr. Piper.

"Prrr!" said Mrs. Cat.

"Why not?" they all seemed to be thinking. "This is a good place. Why go anywhere else?"

"But I thought you all wanted to live in the city," said Mr. Piper.

Buster reached into the hole and pulled out a dirty old bone that some other dog had buried long ago. He walked over and put it in Mr. Piper's lap. Mr. and Mrs. Mack flew up and sat on the porch rail. And Mrs. Cat went after the black kitten, who had started to fall into the hole in the porch again. She picked him up and carried him to Mr. Piper. She had to hold her head high so as not to bump him on the floor. She dumped him at Mr. Piper's feet, as if she were saying, "Here, you mind him. I've got enough to do without pulling him out of that hole all the time."

They all seemed to be trying to tell him something. Suddenly he knew what it was. They didn't care whether they were in the city or the country. They just wanted to be with *him*.

Mr. Piper said, "But don't you see, I have to go back to my job. And I *can't* take you along."

They weren't the least bit interested.

"I guess you just don't understand English," said Mr. Piper. "We'll stay here today. Tomorrow morning, we go on, and that's final. On the way, I'll see if I can find the owner of this place, and pay him for the use of his house."

Meanwhile, he thought, he might as well clean the place up a little. He went inside and found an old broom, and swept the floor. He shook the quilt and aired it on the porch. Then he spread it neatly over the bed. He got some water from the rusty pump in the yard and washed the windows. He cleaned the

fireplace. He found a piece of wood and some nails and fixed the broken board in the porch.

By lunch time, the little house was much cleaner, and Mr. Piper was good and tired. He took a nap. It was late when he woke up. The sun was far over in the west. He went for a walk in the garden. There were raspberries on a bush there, and he picked some for his supper.

After supper, he sat on the porch and smoked his pipe. Two deer came out of the woods across the road. They nibbled grass in the meadow for a while. Then they bounded away among the trees.

The stars came out. Far down in the valley, lights twinkled. Up on the mountain, Mr. Piper sniffed the cool, piney air.

"I'd like to stay here forever," he said. Then he went indoors to bed.

Mr. Piper got up very early the next morning. There was a great deal to do.

"We're leaving," he said to his animals. "Right after breakfast."

But first he had to clean up his bus. He swept it out. He looked in the barn and found a big piece of tar paper, which he nailed over the top of the bus. He hoped the owner would let him pay for it. The job took longer than he thought it would, and before he knew it, it was lunch time.

He looked in the garden and found some tomato vines growing wild, with little red tomatoes on them. There was a cucumber vine with little green cucumbers. Mr. Piper cleaned out the weeds and tied up the vines. He picked some tomatoes and cucumbers for

68

his lunch. There were flowers among the vines, and Mr. Piper picked some and put them in a chipped pitcher on the mantelshelf. They looked very pretty.

"I don't think anybody could mind that," he said.

After lunch, he found an old lawn mower in the shed, and he cut the grass. He picked up the branches that had blown down from the maple tree in the storm.

By then it was time for supper. Mr. Piper never noticed where the day had gone. It was too late now to go looking for the owner of the house. It would have to wait until tomorrow. Oh, well, he thought, it wouldn't hurt to stay one more night.

But at supper time, when he looked into the grocery box, it was nearly empty. There was some coffee and some sugar and a box of oatmeal.

That settled it. Tomorrow morning they would go.

9. Down the Mountain

Mr. Piper drank some coffee and ate some oatmeal for breakfast. He had no milk to go with them. Buster and Mrs. Cat were not interested in coffee and oatmeal. Mrs. Cat went out and caught a mouse, and Buster gnawed on his old bone. They both looked sadly at Mr. Piper, as if they were asking why he couldn't give them a better breakfast.

"I'm sorry," he said. "I explained to you that I had to go back to work, and now you see why."

He began carrying things out to the bus. He was just starting out of the house with his blankets rolled up in his arms, when he heard a noise. It was a very strange noise. It sounded like a giggle!

70

Buster heard it, too. "Woof!" he barked.

Then a voice exclaimed, "Oh, look, a dog!"

"Kittens!" said another voice. "And bantam chickens!"

Mr. Piper put down the blankets and went to the door. Three children stood in the yard. There were two boys and a girl. All of them had light yellow hair and bare feet. They all wore overalls, and they carried pails full of blueberries.

Buster ran to the little girl and licked her bare foot. "*Eeeek!*" she squealed.

71

"Don't be afraid, Polly," said the bigger boy. "He's a nice dog."

"Who are you?" Mr. Piper asked.

"I'm Billy Honeywell," answered the boy. "This is Henry, and this is Polly. We live down yonder. We went berry-picking and saw somebody was here."

The little girl sat down and took the kittens in her lap.

"Don't touch the kittens, Polly," said Billy. "The mother cat might not like it." But Mrs. Cat didn't mind. She seemed to think this girl knew how to hold kittens.

Mr. Piper said, "You can have one if you like. In fact, you can have them all."

Polly shook her head sadly. "We have two cats and four kittens already. Ma wouldn't like any more."

"Would you like to have a dog?" Mr. Piper asked.

Henry shook his head. "No more dogs, Ma said."

Then Polly asked, "Why can't we just play with them here?"

Mr. Piper shook *his* head. "I have to go away now," he explained. "I was just getting ready when you came."

"Oh!" said Henry. "Aren't you going to live here now?"

"No," Mr. Piper told him. "I just came in here because it was raining. I don't even know whose house it is."

"It's our Grandpa's house," said Billy. "But he got real old and came to live with us. Nobody wants it now, Pa says."

"I wish I could stay in it," said Mr. Piper, "but I have to be going. I'd like to speak to your daddy first, though. Is he home?"

"He's in the store, down in the village," said Billy. "We'll show you, if you like."

Mr. Piper picked up his blankets again and started for the bus.

"We'll help you," Billy offered.

"All right," said Mr. Piper. "You may carry the kittens. I have to go and catch the chickens."

Mr. Mack was sitting on the fence, but Mrs. Mack was nowhere to be seen.

"Now where did that hen go?" Mr. Piper wondered. "She was here a minute ago." He went to look in the shed, but she was not there. He searched in the garden. He poked in the weeds with a stick,

73

gently, so as not to hurt her. "I must find her," he said. "I can't go without her."

Suddenly, with a loud squawk, Mrs. Mack came rushing out from behind a bush. She looked very angry.

"I think she wanted to steal a nest," said Billy.

"Steal a nest? What does that mean?" Mr. Piper asked.

Billy laughed. "That's what hens do when they want to set on their eggs and hatch out some chicks, and think you won't let them."

"I'm sorry," said Mr. Piper. "She'll have to do that some other time. Right now she must come with me. Climb in, children, and I'll give you a ride down the mountain."

"That will be fun," said Henry. "I never rode in a bus before."

The children got into the bus and sat happily looking out of the windows. Mr. Piper looked back at the little house, sitting all alone on the side of the mountain. Then he started the bus. Down the stony road they rattled.

"This is fun!" said Polly.

"How come you never rode in a bus before?" Mr. Piper asked.

"They don't run buses here," Billy told him.

"We've never been away," said Henry.

"Where do you go to school?" Mr. Piper asked.

"Oh, our school is way down in the valley," said Billy. "We walk there."

Just then they passed a farmhouse.

"That's our house," Billy said. "Ma isn't home. She's off taking care of somebody who's sick. Pa's in the store. I reckon Grandpa's there, too."

Soon they passed another house. "That's Andy's house," said Billy. "Here comes Andy."

A boy came running out, and Billy explained, "This man was staying in Grandpa's house. We're taking him to the store to see Pa."

"Can I come, too?" Andy asked.

75

"Come on," said Mr. Piper.

Another farmhouse came in sight. All the houses were gray and weather-beaten, as if they had never been painted. They had rough stone chimneys and little porches. There were flowers in the front yards.

Two children stood in the road.

"Those are Mary and George," said Billy. "Can they come, too?"

"All aboard," said Mr. Piper. Mary and George climbed on.

About half a mile farther on, two girls in blue dresses appeared.

"Those are Emily and Ann," said Polly. Mr. Piper

stopped for them, too. Each child sat by a window.

"I never thought I would get to ride in a bus," said Emily.

"I surely do like it," said Ann.

Mr. Piper liked it, too. He loved his animals, but he also liked to have people on board.

"If only I could have both!" he thought. Then he asked, "How much farther is it to the village?"

"This is the village, right here," Billy told him.

Mr. Piper looked around. It was a very small village. There was a church, painted white. There

was an old mill by a creek. There were two houses and a store with a lone gasoline pump in front.

"Yonder's the store," said Billy. "Pa and Grandpa are inside."

Mr. Piper stopped the bus. All the children jumped out and went with him into the store.

10. Home Again

The store was very old. An iron stove stood in the middle of the floor. On the walls were shelves with all kinds of things on them. There were tools, lanterns, rubber boots and rolls of cloth. There was a barrel of flour and a barrel of sugar. There were baskets of eggs and a string of straw hats.

A man stood behind the counter. Two old men sat behind the stove. Three women were shopping. They all turned to look at Mr. Piper and the children.

"This is Pa," said Billy, nodding at the man behind the counter.

"Howdy," said Billy's father. Then he asked the children, "What are all you young'uns doing here?"

Billy looked at Mr. Piper. "We came to show him the way," he explained.

"Mary and George," said one of the women, "I thought I told you to mind the house."

"You, Andy," said another woman, "you got all the kindling cut?"

"No, Ma," said Andy. "But we wanted to ride in the bus."

"Bus! What bus?"

Mr. Piper stepped up to the counter. "It's my bus," he said. "My name is Hiram Piper. I got lost on the mountain. I found an empty house up there and I

80

stayed in it that night it rained so hard. Then I stayed a couple of days longer. Billy says it's his Grandpa's house."

"It is," said Billy's father. "But nobody lives in it now, except mice."

"My cat caught a few of them," said Mr. Piper.

"Mr. Piper fixed the house all up," said Billy. "He cleaned it and mowed the yard and weeded the garden."

"He's got a cat and kittens and a dog and two bantam chickens," said Polly. "He's a nice man." She put her hand in Mr. Piper's and smiled up at him.

"We like him," said Henry. "He rode us down the hill in his bus."

"How come you to be driving a bus?" Mr. Honeywell asked.

"I have an old bus that I've been taking a vacation in," said Mr. Piper. "Vacation's over now, and I have to go home. If any of you people would like a dog, or a cat with four kittens, or two bantam chickens, I'd be pleased to give them away."

Mr. Honeywell shook his head. "We all have more than enough cats and dogs," he answered.

"Couldn't we have the bantams, Pa?" Billy asked.

"Our rooster would fight with the bantam rooster," his father said.

Mr. Piper sighed. "Well, I've got to be going. But first, I want to pay for using your house."

One of the old men behind the stove spoke up. "We don't want to take anything," he said. "If you weeded the garden, that would be enough. I used to set store by that garden. Nobody has time to go up the hill and tend it now, and I'm too old."

"It's a nice house," said Mr. Piper. "I'd like to stay in it if I could. But I can't. I'll get some groceries, and I'll ask you to fill my tank with gas. Then I'll be on my way."

He picked out the groceries he wanted while Mr. Honeywell filled his tank. Then he took out his wallet to pay for what he had bought.

He looked into the wallet in amazement. There was exactly one dollar in it!

What could have happened? Where had all his money gone? How could he get back to the city with only one dollar? Everybody in the store stared at him.

"My money is gone!" exclaimed Mr. Piper.

"You lose it?" George's mother asked.

"I must have spent it," said Mr. Piper. "I thought I had a ten-dollar bill, but it's only a one."

What could he do now? He would have to earn some money before he even started. "Could I do some kind of work here?" he asked.

"Can you milk a cow?" Mr. Honeywell asked.

Mr. Piper shook his head.

"Kin you pitch hay?" said Andy's mother. "We got haying to do."

"No, I can't. That is, I never have. I suppose I could try.

83

"Well, what can you do?" Grandpa Honeywell asked.

Mr. Piper said, "The only thing I can do is drive a bus. That's why I have to go back to the city. That's my job."

"We don't have much need for a bus here," said Mr. Honeywell.

"Yes, we do!" said Billy, suddenly.

"What for?" his father asked.

"To take us kids to school," said Billy, "so we don't have to walk all that way. School starts day after tomorrow."

The other children all began to talk at once. "Yes, we want a bus to take us to school."

"All the other kids come in a bus."

"Why can't we?"

"But where would we get a bus?" one of the women asked.

"He's got a bus," said Billy. "It's right there. He can ride us to school."

The women looked at each other and nodded. "It's a good idea," said George's mother. "If we had a bus, the menfolks wouldn't have to ride the kids to school in bad weather."

"That's right. And it's too far for little ones to

84

walk, even in good weather," said Andy's mother.

Grandpa Honeywell said nothing, but the other old man said, "New-fangled nonsense. In my young days, we walked to school."

"You're way behind the times," exclaimed Andy's mother. "Nowadays, kids ride to school. The only thing is, how could this village pay a bus driver?"

"I could give him eggs and milk," said George's mother.

"I could give him his groceries," said Mr. Honeywell.

"He could have my house to live in," said Grandpa Honeywell, "and maybe we could all pay a little. A man needs *some* money."

The other old man said, grumpily, "Well, if you're all giving something, I'll pay for the gas. Nobody can say *my* grandchildren couldn't afford to ride on a bus."

Emily and Ann ran to him and hugged him. "Thank you, Grandpa," they said.

Mr. Piper said nothing. He just looked surprised and pleased. Everybody in the store waited to hear what he had to say.

Finally, Grandpa Honeywell asked, "Well, young

feller, what do you say? Do you want to drive our young'uns to school?"

"I'd like to," said Mr. Piper. "How long would you want me to stay? I can't take much more time off from my job."

"We want you to stay for *good!*" Billy exclaimed.

"That's what we've been saying," Grandpa Honeywell told him.

For a minute Mr. Piper couldn't speak. Then he stammered, "You—you mean, stay here? *Live* here?"

"Sure enough," said Mr. Honeywell. "Stay as long as you want to."

Mr. Piper looked around at all their friendly faces. He looked out at his animals, waiting for him in the bus. He could stay in the little house! He could keep the animals!

"I'll do it!" he shouted.

He took the dollar out of his wallet. "I want to send a telegram," he said. "No, I'll write a letter. It will be cheaper."

He bought a sheet of paper and a stamp and envelope. Then, leaning on the counter, he wrote a letter to his boss.

"Sorry, I'm not coming back," he wrote. "Family business is settled. I must stay here to take care of it."

86

Then he remembered his landlady. He wrote her a letter, too. "Not coming back, ever," he said. "Yours truly, H. Piper. P.S. You may keep the television set."

"Now that everything's settled," he said, "I'll go back home." He said "home" in a very special way, thinking of the snug little house on the mountain. "The day after tomorrow, I'll be ready to take the children to school."

"There's just one thing," Billy said.

"Yes? What is it?" his father asked.

"Mr. Piper's bus is green, and a school bus ought to be yellow," said Billy.

"You're too fussy, young man," said his father.

But Mr. Piper said, "He's right. I should fix it up. I must buy some paint. Only—I don't think I have enough money."

"Wait," said Mr. Honeywell. "Here is a big can of yellow paint. It's been here for pretty near five years. Nobody bought it because it's too bright."

"Can't see what you ever got it for," said Grandpa Honeywell. "Nobody paints their houses yellow."

"I can't see that anybody around here paints their houses at all," said Emily and Ann's grandpa, grumpily.

"Well, it's just right for a bus," said Mr. Honeywell.

Mr. Piper took the paint. With the rest of his money he bought a brush. Then he drove happily back up the mountain, dropping the children off at their houses. When he got to his own little house, he opened the door of the bus.

Buster and Mrs. Cat jumped out. Mr. and Mrs. Mack flew out.

"We're going to stay here," Mr. Piper told them.

They didn't seem at all surprised. They acted as though they had known it all along.

Mr. Piper carried his chair and table into the house.

He put his dishes on the shelves and hung his pots and pans over the stove. He spread his blankets on the bed.

"It looks like home," he said.

Suddenly, from behind the house, he heard a loud cackling and squawking. "Cut-cut-cudaaa-cut!"

Had something happened? Mr. Piper hurried out to the shed. Everything was quite all right. There sat Mrs. Mack on her nest.

"Cut-cut-cut-cudaaa-cut!" she cackled again.

89

"What! You laid another egg?" said Mr. Piper. "Well, that's fine. Congratulations! But why do you have to make so much noise about it?"

He felt under her warm feathers. But when he tried to take the egg out of the nest, she pecked at his hand angrily.

Mr. Piper laughed. "All right, all right, you may keep it. I hope you lay plenty of them and they all hatch. But excuse me now, I have work to do."

He went to work on the bus. If it was going to be a school bus, it had to be spick and span. He washed it, inside and out. He polished the windows. He cleaned the engine and tested the brakes. A school bus had to be safe.

Then he painted it yellow. On each side he painted the words: SCHOOL BUS.

Bright and early on the first day of school, Mr. Piper was up. He fed his animals. He put on his bus-driver's uniform and cap. He climbed in behind the wheel. Buster jumped up beside him. Down the hill went the shining yellow bus. At each house, boys and girls got in.

Proudly they took their seats, and they all set out for the school down in the valley.

Mr. Piper began to sing:

> "She'll be comin' round the mountain
>   when she comes!
> She'll be comin' round the mountain
>   when she comes!"

And the boys and girls joined in.

> "She'll be comin' round the mountain,
> She'll be comin' round the mountain,

91

She'll be comin' round the mountain
when she comes!"

After that it was quiet in the bus for a while. Mr. Piper thought he could hear the children whispering behind him, but he couldn't hear what they were saying. And then, suddenly, they burst out, singing as loudly as they could:

"We are ridin' down the mountain—
look at us!
We are ridin' down the mountain—
look at us!
We are ridin' down the mountain,
We are ridin' down the mountain,
We are ridin' down *in Mis-ter Pi-per's
BUS!*"

ELEANOR CLYMER

has lived most of her life in New York, with intervals for travel and study. She graduated from the University of Wisconsin and studied at Bank Street College, New York University and Teachers College. A successful author in other fields, she began writing for children when her son was old enough to listen to stories. Her first book, *A Yard for John*, was the story of a child's wish for a place where he would have plenty of room for play, and her many subsequent books also reflected her feeling for children's many needs and interests.

3088